SUMI'S
First Day of School Ever

By SOYUNG PAK

Illustrated by JOUNG UN KIM

VIKING

VIKING
Published by the Penguin Group
Penguin Putnam Books for Young Readers, 345 Hudson Street, New York, New York 10014, U.S.A.
Penguin Books Ltd, 80 Strand, London WC2R 0RL, England
Penguin Books Australia Ltd, 250 Camberwell Road, Camberwell, Victoria 3124, Australia
Penguin Books Canada Ltd, 10 Alcorn Avenue, Toronto, Ontario, Canada M4V 3B2
Penguin Books (N.Z.) Ltd, 182-190 Wairau Road, Auckland 10, New Zealand

Penguin Books Ltd, Registered Offices: Harmondsworth, Middlesex, England

First published in 2003 by Viking, a division of Penguin Putnam Books for Young Readers.

1 3 5 7 9 10 8 6 4 2

LIBRARY OF CONGRESS CATALOGING-IN-PUBLICATION DATA
Pak, Soyung.
Sumi's first day of school ever / by Soyung Pak ; illustrated by
Joung Un Kim.
p. cm.
Summary: By the time Sumi finishes her first day of school, she decides
that school is not as lonely, scary, or mean as she had thought.
ISBN 0-670-03522-X (hardcover)
[1. First day of school—Fiction. 2. Schools—Fiction. 3. Korean
Americans—Fiction.] I. Kim, Joung Un, ill. II. Title.
PZ7.P173 Su 2003
[E]—dc21
2002011309

Manufactured in China
Set in Avenir
Book design by Nancy Brennan

On Sumi's first day of school, her mother taught her two things. Sumi's mother taught her what people said when they wanted to know her name, and she taught Sumi how to say it.

"Hello, what is your name?" Sumi's mother asked.

"Hello, my name is Sumi," Sumi answered.

They practiced all morning as Sumi dressed, then they practiced during their walk to school.

When they arrived at school, Sumi saw the big building.
Sumi saw the children. Some of them were big.
She saw the wide stairs and the tall metal fence.

Sumi held on to her mother's hand as they walked into Sumi's class. Then Sumi's mother let Sumi's hand go and said good-bye. As Sumi saw her mother walk away, she thought, *School is a lonely place.*

Sumi looked around. She saw a blackboard.

She saw rows of desks and didn't know where to sit.

She saw lots of children who were loud and noisy and saying things she didn't understand.

School is a scary place, Sumi thought as she stood near the door, not knowing what to do.

When the teacher pointed to a seat, Sumi sat in it.

When the other children in the class stood up, so did Sumi.

And when they sat down again, Sumi sat down, too.

A boy stuck out his tongue. He made a noise. He squished his eyes.

School is a mean place, Sumi thought.

SUNDAY
MONDAY
TUESDAY
1
2

But then the teacher talked to the boy. Afterwards, he turned to Sumi.

He said something. She could tell he was saying something nice, even though she didn't know what it was.

The teacher patted Sumi's head, just like Sumi's mother. When the teacher looked into Sumi's eyes, the teacher smiled until Sumi smiled, too.

Maybe school is not so mean, Sumi thought, as she listened to her teacher teach.

When the teacher passed out paper, Sumi began to draw.

When Sumi finished, the teacher took her drawing and hung it on the wall.

Maybe school is not so scary, Sumi thought.

During recess, everyone went outside.
There were swings and slides, and balls to bounce.
Sumi found some dirt to draw in.
She found a stick to draw with.

Soon a girl sat down and started drawing, too.
Sumi drew a cat.
The girl drew a dog.
Sumi drew a house.
The girl drew flowers and a sun.

Maybe school is not so lonely, Sumi thought.

"Hello, my name is Mary," the little girl said, as they walked back into the class. "What is your name?"

"My name is Sumi," Sumi answered, just like her mother taught her.

And on Sumi's very first day of school ever, she and her new friend Mary walked back into the not-so-lonely, not-so-scary, not-so-mean class together.